Charles M. Schulz

Beware of the Snoring Ghost!

HarperHorizon
An Imprint of HarperCollins*Publishers*

First published in 1998 by HarperCollins*Publishers* Inc. http://www.harpercollins.com. Copyright © 1998 United Feature Syndicate, Inc. All rights reserved. HarperCollins ® and ♨ ® are trademarks of HarperCollins*Publishers* Inc. *Beware of the Snoring Ghost!* was published by HarperHorizon, an imprint of HarperCollins*Publishers* Inc., 10 East 53rd Street, New York, NY 10022. Horizon is a registered trademark used under license from Forbes Inc. PEANUTS is a registered trademark of United Feature Syndicate, Inc. PEANUTS © United Feature Syndicate, Inc. Based on the PEANUTS ® comic strip by Charles M. Schulz. http://www.unitedmedia.com. ISBN 0-694-01031-6. Printed in Hong Kong.

"Today is report card day, Marcie. Today we find out if we move up a grade."

"I failed?"

"I failed, Marcie! I won't be in your class next year. You won't be sitting behind me."

"Who's going to wake you up when you fall asleep at your desk?"

"When we have tests, who's going to give you all the answers?"

"You never gave me any answers, Marcie!"

"School starts tomorrow, Sir. Are you ready?"

"I'm ready, Marcie. I already know all the answers."

"You didn't know many last year."

"So this year trues will be false and falses will be true!"

"You're weird, Sir!"

"If you need any help, Eudora, I'm right here. I took all of these subjects last year, so I know all the answers. Just do what I do, Eudora, and you'll get along great!"

"It doesn't seem right not having Peppermint Patty sitting in the desk in front of me."

"Now, all I have are memories.
Nothing but ghostly memories."

"Hear it, Franklin?"

"Ma'am? Excuse me, but I think there's something you should hear."

"It's not often you see a teacher turn pale and run out of the room."

"And I told the teacher to listen. She heard it, too."

"She called in the principal, and we all stood around your desk and listened. We could hear your snoring, Sir. It was weird."

"I don't have to listen to this, Marcie."

"What's going on?"

"They're tearing the roof off our school."

"They think that snoring sound above your old desk comes from the air conditioning."

"The kids call it the 'Snoring Ghost.' No one wants to go into the building. I think it's all very amusing, Sir."

"Because you're so weird, Marcie!"

"Yes, Sir, Mr. Principal. I understand. My teacher wants me back with my old class."

"Yes, Sir, I'll study real hard."

"No, Sir, I don't know how a desk can snore without me in it."

"It was our teacher's idea, Marcie. Something made her decide to give me another chance."